DIGGER'S TREASURE

BOOKS IN THE PUPPY PATROL SERIES ™

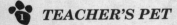

COMING SOON

DIGGER'S TREASURE

JENNY DALE

Illustrations by Mick Reid
Cover illustration by Michael Rowe

AN
APPLE
PAPERBACK

SCHOLASTIC INC.
New York Toronto London Auckland Sydney
Mexico City New Delhi Hong Kong Buenos Aires

SPECIAL THANKS TO LORNA READ

ISBN 0-439-45353-4

12 11 10 9 8 7 6 5 4 3 2 1   3 4 5 6 7 8/0

Printed in the U.S.A.   40
First Scholastic printing, July 2003

CHAPTER ONE

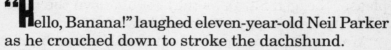

"**H**ello, Banana!" laughed eleven-year-old Neil Parker as he crouched down to stroke the dachshund.

"What a name! How in the world did she get that?" asked his younger sister Emily.

"Well, I guess she *is* sort of long and yellow," Neil replied, looking down at Banana's golden coat. Banana was lying stretched out on the sunny doorstep of her home in the small town of Padsham. Five-year-old Sarah Parker sat down next to her and giggled as the dog gave her a friendly lick on the chin.

"How long would you like us to walk her for?" Neil asked Mrs. Mitchell, her owner.

"Take your time," replied the crisp, businesslike woman. "I won't be back for an hour and a half, but I'll leave you a key so you can let her back in if she gets tired." She handed Neil Banana's leash. He clipped it on and gently encouraged the dachshund to her feet.

Mrs. Mitchell watched with interest as Neil introduced Banana to Jake, his young Border collie. Jake bent his head down to meet the other dog's, his tail wagging politely as they touched noses.

"She gets along well with other dogs, as you can see. So I don't think you'll have any trouble with her," said Mrs. Mitchell. "Now, I really must get to my meeting."

"And we should be off to the Thomsons' house to pick up Digger," said Neil, matching her brisk tone.

"I can't wait to see Digger again. Can I walk him, please?" begged Sarah as they set off down the road. "He's the best puppy in the whole world! I love him."

"We know you do, Squirt," said Neil, remembering how attached Sarah had become to the mongrel puppy after she had helped to rescue him. They had found him stuck in a badger burrow when he was a tiny puppy, and had never been able to trace his owners. Digger had a great new home with the Thomsons now, but Sarah had been heartbroken when she'd had to part with the puppy.

Like their younger sister, Neil and Emily were obsessed with dogs. Luckily for them, their parents ran King Street Kennels, a boarding kennel and rescue center in the market town of Compton, not far from Padsham.

"Here we are." Neil halted by a red gate. "Emily,

you'd better keep Banana here while I go in. Even though Mrs. Mitchell says Banana's OK with other dogs, we can't afford to take chances. I hope she and Digger *do* hit it off, otherwise we'll have to walk them separately."

Jake trotted after Neil and Sarah down the path, staying obediently by his side. "Sit, boy," Neil said, and rang the bell.

Liam Thomson opened the door for them and reached down eagerly to rub Jake's ears. He laughed as the black-and-white Border collie licked his freckled face. Liam was nine and in the grade below Emily's at Meadowbank School in Compton.

Mrs. Thomson appeared behind him and dumped a large bag in the hallway. "Hello, Neil. Hi, Sarah. We're off to my sister's for the day to meet her new baby," she said. "She certainly can't cope with a lively puppy right now. Digger!" she called.

The kitchen door was nudged open and a black-and-tan puppy with a snow-white chest ran down the hallway, yapping excitedly. Sarah squealed and ran to cuddle him. The pup obviously remembered Sarah and jumped all over her, giving little yelps of pleasure. His coat shone with health. *He really is a great-looking dog*, thought Neil.

"Hey, Jake, here's an old friend of yours," he said. Digger gave an excited bark. Jake whined and thumped his tail, then jumped up and rubbed noses with the mongrel puppy.

"They remember each other, don't they?" said Sarah.

"Looks like it." Neil watched as the puppy sniffed Jake. "Digger's really grown since I last saw him."

"Well, he certainly eats a lot!" Mrs. Thomson laughed. She kneeled down beside the puppy and clipped on his leash. "I'm so grateful to you for looking after him this morning — and for offering to walk him over the next couple of weeks," she said. "It's a weight off my mind. At his age, he needs all the exercise he can get, but I'm totally overworked these days."

"No problem," said Neil.

They said good-bye to Mrs. Thomson and Liam, and Sarah proudly led Digger out of the house.

Banana backed away when she saw the puppy approaching. "It's OK, girl," Emily said soothingly, giving her a stroke. She took hold of Banana's collar and kept on stroking her and talking to her while Neil introduced her to Digger.

The mongrel's reaction was to roll over on the sidewalk, exposing his plump white tummy. Banana stared at him, then visibly relaxed and sniffed Digger all over. Neil and Emily looked at each other and grinned. Everything was going to be fine.

"Let's take them to Padsham Castle," Neil suggested. "We haven't been there in a while, and the dogs will love it."

Padsham Castle was a famous local landmark. It looked medieval, with its turrets and drawbridge, but it wasn't actually that old. It had been built a hundred years ago on the site of an ancient castle and now housed a local history museum.

It was a hot Tuesday morning in July, and the gray bulk of the castle, with its square battlements, stood out against the clear blue sky. As soon as they reached the double gates that led into the castle grounds, Neil and Emily let the three dogs off their leashes. The grassy lawns sloped up toward the castle in a gentle hill. Jake and Digger raced ahead, excited by the open space. Neil and Sarah ran after

them, and Emily followed with Banana, whose little legs weren't quite so well adapted for hills. In fact, the dachshund didn't appear to like exercise at all, and kept sitting down and refusing to budge.

"Come on, be a good girl," Emily coaxed when Banana sat down for the fourth time.

Suddenly, a Frisbee bounced through the air and hit Neil on the back of his head. "Ouch!" he cried, rubbing his head. "Who threw that?"

"Hi, Neil!" called a familiar voice. Hasheem Lindon, Neil's school friend, came running up to them. "Sorry about that!"

"I should have known!" Neil laughed.

"Hello, Jake, my old friend." Hasheem kneeled down and rubbed Jake's sides, grinning when the Border collie licked his nose. "And who else have you got here?" he said. "Introduce me to the crew."

While Hasheem fussed over Banana and Digger, Neil told him all about the mongrel puppy.

"I can't believe anyone would abandon a cool pup like him," said Hasheem. "He's going to be a big dog when he grows up. Look at the size of those paws!"

"Yeah, Dad says he's probably got some mountain dog in him," Neil said.

"So how come you're walking Digger *and* Banana?" asked Hasheem.

"We're earning money for a birthday present fund," Emily explained.

"You're so thoughtful! Mine's not till November, so

you've got plenty of time to save," Hasheem joked. "Seriously, though, whose birthday are you saving up for?"

"Our parents'," Neil explained. "Their birthdays are only two days apart. We want to get them an aerial photograph of King Street Kennels."

"Great idea," said Hasheem.

"Yeah, but it's expensive, so Em and I also had the great idea of walking dogs for people over summer vacation, to earn some money. We made some calls and found Digger and Banana."

"Don't Liam and his little sister, Fiona, want to walk Digger themselves?" asked Hasheem.

"Well, they're younger than us," Neil reminded him. "They're not really old enough to be responsible for a puppy on their own. Plus Mrs. Thomson's got no time to go out with them because her sister just had a baby."

"And Mrs. Mitchell works really long hours, so she was more than happy to let us walk Banana," Emily said.

"Well, good luck," said Hasheem, snatching up his Frisbee. "I hope they're not too much of a handful. I'd better get going. I'm on my way back from my Grandma's — Mom will kill me if I'm late. See you."

"Come on, let's give these three a good game of catch to wear them out," suggested Neil when Hasheem had gone.

Digger and Jake were ready to play, but Banana

was reluctant to join in. The dachshund made a couple of feeble runs after the ball, then gave up and flopped down on the grass.

"I just don't understand why she keeps doing that," said Emily.

"Maybe she's lazy and doesn't like going uphill," suggested Neil. "If Mrs. Mitchell doesn't take her out much, she's probably not in very good shape."

"I'm too hot," Sarah complained, sinking down next to Banana. "I'm going to have my candy bar." She took it out of her pocket, unwrapped the foil packaging, and discovered that the chocolate coating had melted in the heat.

Banana stuck her nose into the air and sniffed eagerly, scenting the chocolate. "Don't give her any, Sarah. Chocolate's bad for dogs," Emily reminded her sister.

Neil took a bottle of water and a plastic bowl from his backpack and gave each dog a drink. When the bowl was placed in front of Digger, he put his paw in it. The dish tipped up and water splashed all over the surprised pup.

"Digger just took a shower." Sarah giggled as her brother filled up the bowl again.

After a break, they made their way down the hill toward the gates, then back onto the public land that bordered the castle walls.

"Phew!" said Neil, wiping his forehead. "It's going

to be hard work walking these three every day for the next two weeks — especially in this heat."

"Yeah, but it will be worth it if we raise enough money for the photo," said Emily. "And Sarah loves it. She's been following Digger everywhere!"

"Hey, Digger! Stop that!" Neil called as he spotted the puppy scratching furiously in the dry dirt beneath a bush. "Come here, boy. I'd better put his leash on, Sarah. We don't want him running off after rabbits."

"I'll get him," Sarah offered. She crouched down beside the bush and reached for Digger's collar. But before she could grab it, the ground seemed to sag beneath her. She lost her footing and screamed. Then, to Neil and Emily's astonishment, the earth gave way completely and Sarah and Digger disappeared from sight. . . .

CHAPTER TWO

"**S**arah? Are you OK?" Emily called anxiously as they ran toward the spot where they had last seen their sister and Digger.

Jake got there first. He began barking loudly, and the next moment they heard Sarah's tearful voice calling, "Help me! Get me out! I've fallen down a hole!"

"Don't worry, Squirt, we'll get you out," reassured Neil as he peered down into the hole, careful not to get too close to its crumbling edge. It looked as though a thin crust of soil beneath the bush had collapsed into a sort of trench. It was a yard or so deep. Sarah was sitting on a muddy pile of dirt and stones in the middle of it, holding her knee.

"I'm b-bleeding," she said in a wobbly voice.

"Where's Digger?" Emily asked, peering down into the gloom.

"I don't know!" Sarah wailed.

"Maybe he ran away when the ground collapsed," Neil said. "Digger! Digger!"

There was a muffled bark from a dingy corner of the hole and the pup emerged into the half-light, shaking dirt and dust from his coat.

"He's OK. What a relief," said Neil.

"Get me out!" Sarah cried again.

"Lift Digger up and pass him to me, then we'll get you out, Squirt," Neil said, looking down at her muddy, tear-stained face.

Sarah tried to pick up Digger, but the puppy gave an excited yap and struggled free, eager to return to his tunneling.

Neil groaned. "Oh, great! I think he *likes* being in holes," he said. "OK. Let's get *you* out first, Sarah, so we can clean up that knee of yours. Reach up and I'll see if I can grab you."

Sarah's head was below ground level. She raised her arms, and Neil lay on his stomach on the ground and reached down toward her. But his arms weren't long enough, and their hands couldn't quite make contact.

"Give me a dog leash, Em!" Neil held one hand out behind him and Emily took Banana's leash out of her jeans pocket and gave it to him. Neil coiled the leash around his hand, kneeled down, and threw the other end to Sarah, who caught hold of it.

"Hold on tight," Neil ordered.

He pulled as hard as he could, but it was no use. Sarah didn't have a strong enough grip and each time he tugged, the thin leash just slipped through her hands.

He gave up. "I think we'd better get help. You stay here with Banana and Jake, Em. I'll run to the castle and find someone."

"Don't leave me here on my own!" Sarah sobbed.

"It's OK, Sarah, I'm here," reassured Emily.

Neil set off toward the entrance of the castle grounds. As he was approaching the gate, a car honked. "Hello, Neil," said a voice. Neil spun around. It was the first time in his life he actually felt relieved to see his teacher.

"I was just on my way to the archaeological dig behind the castle. I'm working there, helping Professor Tate," Mr. Hamley explained. "Would you like a ride?"

"No, thanks. What I really need is help. Sarah fell down a hole, and we can't get her out," Neil explained urgently.

Mr. Hamley parked his car on the grassy shoulder of the road and got out. He was dressed in khaki shorts and an old, faded T-shirt instead of his usual teacher clothes. "OK. Take me to Sarah," he said, and quickly followed Neil.

"Mr. Hamley!" cried Emily in surprise as she saw them approach.

"Hello, Emily. Hold on, Sarah, you'll be out of there in no time," Mr. Hamley called soothingly. As he walked carefully toward the edge of the hole, a loud yap came out of it. "There's a dog down there, too?" he said.

"It's Digger — Liam and Fiona Thomson's puppy," Emily explained. Neil peered down and saw Sarah cuddling him.

"Those look like the foundations of a house to me," Mr. Hamley said, looking at the stones Sarah was sitting on. "Sarah, could you lift Digger up to me, please?"

The teacher lay on his stomach on the ground, like Neil had done. His arms were stronger than Neil's and could reach much farther, but Digger had a mind of his own. He didn't want to go to Mr. Hamley, either. He wriggled free from Sarah's grasp again, scrabbled in the loose soil, and vanished into the gloom.

Mr. Hamley sighed. "We'll have to get him out later. Come on, Sarah. Let me take your wrists. I won't hurt you. There's a big rock there. See if you can get your foot on it when I pull." Slowly and carefully, he eased Sarah out of the hole and placed her gently back on firm ground. "There you are," he said kindly. "You're safe now. Are you all right?"

She had lost a shoe and was absolutely filthy, but apart from the cut on her knee and a few grazes and bruises, she hadn't done herself any serious damage.

"I ripped my shorts," she said grumpily as Emily hugged her.

"Never mind. Let's have a look at that knee of yours." Mr. Hamley produced a clean handkerchief and wrapped it around Sarah's knee. "Now, how are we going to get this dog out?" he said.

"Here, Digger!" Neil ordered.

Digger was busy excavating a hole between two rocks. Neil made his voice as commanding as possible, so that the pup would have no doubt that he should obey right away.

"Digger! Come here! Up!" Neil patted his leg. Digger gave him a mischievous look, turned his back, and returned to his digging activities. Soft dirt flew up between his legs, and Neil couldn't help but laugh.

As they watched, the dog's excavations reached a frantic pitch and suddenly stopped. Digger gave a little whine, then turned and bounded to the front of the hole, carrying something in his mouth and wagging his tail like crazy.

"It looks like Digger found a bone." Mr. Hamley laughed.

"Digger, come here." Neil clapped his hands. This time the puppy scrambled out willingly. He promptly shook himself, showering Neil with soil.

"Yuck!" he said, brushing himself off. "Let's see what you've got. Drop it, boy!"

The bone-shaped object was about twenty inches long and covered in hard-packed soil. Digger obediently placed it at Neil's feet, and Jake trotted up and sniffed it. Curiously, Neil picked it up and turned it over a few times. "It's shaped like a bone, but it's not a real one — it's way too heavy," he said. "I'm not sure what it is."

Emily craned her neck for a look. "Maybe it's just a piece of old wood," she suggested.

"No. It's harder than wood. What do you think, Mr. Hamley?" He handed the object to his teacher. Mr. Hamley took some keys out of his pocket and started scratching at the dirt, but stopped abruptly. "I don't want to damage it," he said, handing it back to Neil.

"It feels like metal to me. Lead, or perhaps copper. But I think Professor Tate should take a look at it. Keep it safe in your backpack for now."

"Where is the dig?" asked Neil.

"Just behind the castle. The professor and a team from her university are excavating the original Norman foundations. Weren't you at that talk she gave at school?"

"Uh, yes, I was," Neil replied sheepishly. He hadn't been very interested in Norman castles and couldn't remember much about her project. But the professor's story about a dog-loving baron in the Middle Ages who'd kept Irish wolfhounds in the castle had caught his attention.

"We could show it to her right now," Emily suggested eagerly. "It might be important."

"I think we should get Sarah home first," Mr. Hamley said.

"You're right," agreed Neil. "But how can we? Dad's not picking us up for another half an hour."

"I'll drive Sarah back to King Street Kennels and tell your parents what happened. Then I'll meet you at the dig in twenty minutes," offered Mr. Hamley. "You can give those dogs some more exercise while I'm gone. I'd better report this hole to the authorities, too, so that it can be made safe. And if Digger's dug up anything interesting, Professor Tate might want to investigate the site."

Under normal circumstances, the last thing Neil

would have wanted to do was spend time with "Smiler," as Neil's class called his teacher, especially over summer vacation, but this occasion was different. Mr. Hamley was off-duty and besides, Neil wanted to find out more about the object Digger had unearthed. Maybe it was something valuable. Perhaps they'd get a reward for finding it, which they could put into the fund for their parents' birthday present. They weren't earning a lot from walking the dogs, so anything extra would be a big help.

After Mr. Hamley and Sarah had gone, Neil and Emily dusted Digger down as much as they could. The dirty pup would need a bath, and they would have a lot of explaining to do to Mrs. Thomson!

"We'd better put Jake and Digger on their leashes now. We don't want them disturbing the soil at the dig," Neil said as he and Emily walked behind the castle and approached the cordoned-off area where a team of archaeologists were busy at work. Banana, on the other hand, was very unlikely to interfere. The dachshund had sat down twice on their walk back up the hill — Neil had made a mental note to mention her to the local vet, Mike Turner.

"There's the professor. I recognize her from school," said Emily, pointing to a short figure whose auburn hair was held back from her forehead by a leopard-print headband. She was wearing grubby denim overalls and a red T-shirt. On her feet were big, clumpy boots, covered in caked-on dirt.

They stood and watched the men and women methodically working their way around the site with their delicate tools until Mr. Hamley returned.

"Professor Tate!" he called. "I'd like to introduce you to Neil and Emily Parker. They've got something interesting to tell you."

When Neil told the professor about the hole, she smiled delightedly. "I've had a theory for some time that there were some twelfth-century Norman houses near the castle," she told Neil and Emily. "Perhaps your sister fell into the foundations of one of them. She might have done us a big favor. If those *are* the foundations, it could have taken us months to find them."

"You can thank Digger, too," Emily said. "He was the one who wanted to sniff around that particular bush!"

"He's a cute dog," the professor said admiringly. She gave his broad forehead a stroke and received a wet lick on her muddy wrist.

Neil had saved the best till last. "There is one more thing," he said. "While Digger was in the hole, he found something. This . . ."

He took the bone-shaped object carefully out of his backpack and handed it to the professor. She touched it gently, then took a small, stiff brush from one of her pockets and began to flick away the dust. Neil, Emily, and Mr. Hamley crowded around to see what she was doing. As Neil watched, he saw a faint golden gleam appear.

Professor Tate caught her breath. She glanced up at them, her vivid blue eyes sparkling with excitement. "I think we've really got something here," she said. "I'll have to clean it up and carry out some tests on it, but if I'm not mistaken, Digger's bone is made of gold!"

CHAPTER THREE

"**D**on't get your hopes up," Bob Parker warned as they sat around the big kitchen table at King Street Kennels that evening, discussing the bone. "There are several things that resemble gold at a glance. Brass, for instance."

"But this was really *old,* Dad! Did they have brass in those days?" Emily asked.

"I don't know, but I'm sure Professor Tate would be able to tell you," said Carole Parker.

"Do you think there's a buried treasure in the hole I fell down?" asked Sarah.

"You can ask Professor Tate tomorrow," Neil said.

"I can't wait!" said Sarah impatiently.

The professor had called earlier that evening to invite the Parkers to the museum the next morning.

She said she had some exciting news for them, but wouldn't tell them anything more on the phone.

Sarah was not the only one who couldn't wait for tomorrow. That evening was one of the longest Neil had ever experienced. Despite the fact that one of his favorite animal rescue shows was on television, he felt restless and impatient.

In the end, he whistled for Jake, who jumped at the opportunity for yet another walk. "You can never get enough exercise, can you, boy?" Neil said fondly, ruffling the young collie's rough, wavy fur. Jake nudged his wet nose into Neil's hand, as if to say, *You're right*.

Carole drove them all to Padsham Castle the next morning. Jake traveled in the dog carrier in the back of the car, and he soon had Banana and Digger for company; they picked them up on the way to the castle. Despite all the excitement of finding the bone, the dogs still had to be walked.

"Five to eleven. Perfect timing," Carole Parker said as she brought their Range Rover to a halt in the parking lot.

Neil opened the back and Jake jumped out, followed by Digger. Banana wouldn't budge and had to be lifted. As they walked toward the castle, a familiar figure waved to them from the museum entrance. The smiling, gray-haired lady had a small terrier next to her. It was standing on its hind legs and bouncing around as if it were dancing.

"I can see Mrs. Jones and Toby!" Sarah said excitedly, rushing up to pet the terrier.

Maggie Jones, the castle caretaker, and Toby, her terrier, lived in a cottage on the grounds of Padsham Castle. Maggie sold entrance tickets to the museum, and souvenirs and refreshments in the shop.

"Hello, all. So which of these wonderful creatures is the famous Digger?" asked Mrs. Jones.

"This one here." Neil scratched the mongrel behind one floppy ear. Digger gazed up at Neil. He looked as if he were about to tell the story of finding the golden bone himself.

Dogs weren't allowed in the museum, so Mrs. Jones offered to look after Digger, Banana, and Jake in her shop.

Neil's heart thumped with excitement as he spotted Professor Tate waiting for them by the ticket desk. What she had to say was obviously meant for their ears only. She whisked them into a side room that was equipped like a small lecture hall, with chairs, tables, and a chalkboard.

"Nice to meet you, Mrs. Parker," she said, holding out a hand.

"Call me Carole, please," Carole Parker said.

"And you must call me Vicki. Your children are honored guests in Padsham Castle today," she said, before turning to Neil, Emily, and Sarah. "I've already told my university department all about your finds. I've contacted the local paper, too. They want to do an article on how you found the bone, if that's OK with you?"

"Great!" said Neil.

"Jake Fielding from the *Compton News* should be here any minute," the professor continued. "Now, I know you're all dying to hear about the bone Digger found, but I don't want to say anything until Mr. Fielding gets here. That way, I won't have to tell it all twice!"

Just then, the professor was interrupted by the sound of a car pulling up, followed by a frenzied outburst of barking outside the window. Emily grinned. "That sounds like Jake now!"

Moments later, the tall, ponytailed figure of Jake Fielding, photographer and reporter with the *Compton News,* strode through the door and introduced himself to Vicki Tate. Neil and Emily knew him well. He'd written lots of articles on King Street Kennels and was always happy to feature rescued dogs who urgently needed new homes. His appealing pictures and write-ups had solved many a lonely, unwanted pup's problem.

"Now that you're here, Jake, I'll run briefly through the background story for you. Then, later, you can ask Neil, Emily, and Sarah any questions you want to," Vicki Tate said.

Jake Fielding switched on his tape recorder. "I'm going to syndicate this story to the national press, too," he said with a smile. "I think people all over the country might be interested in this find."

Professor Tate unrolled a map of the grounds of Padsham Castle. "The shaded areas represent where we've dug so far. Here . . . and here . . . are the places where we've found Norman remains. This red patch outside the boundary, on the public land, is where Digger found the bone."

She rolled up the map and put it down on the table next to a wooden box. "Do you remember when I visited your school and told you the story about the baron who lived here in the Middle Ages and loved dogs?" she asked.

Neil and Emily nodded. "You said he kept wolfhounds," Neil said.

"What a good memory!" Vicki Tate smiled. "Now I'll tell you something really exciting," she went on. "Recently, I discovered a rare manuscript that refers to the Baron of Padsham. It appears he was a real person, not just a legend."

"Wow!" exclaimed Emily.

"But that's not all," the professor added. Neil leaned forward and held his breath. "I took another look at the manuscript yesterday — just to see if it would give me any clues about Digger's find. It says that when the baron's last and favorite dog died, he was so heartbroken that he took all the toys and mementos of his dogs and put them away. He had no heirs to leave them to and he couldn't bear to have them around him, reminding him of the dogs."

"Aah," Sarah sighed, enthralled by the story.

"Did he hide them in the castle?" asked Carole.

"Apparently not," said the professor. "He was afraid of the items being stolen, so he hid them in the house of a friend of his, where nobody would think to search. Apparently, his friend lived just outside the castle grounds — which is where Digger found the bone." She paused and looked around expectantly, before adding, "The manuscript says that many of the items were made of gold and precious stones!"

Excited conversation broke out among the Parkers. Professor Tate held up her hand for silence, her round face all smiles.

"I've kept quiet about the manuscript up until now and I'm sure you can understand why. If its contents had become known to the public, we'd have had treasure hunters with metal detectors digging holes all over the place. But now the cat, or rather the bone, is out of the bag!" the professor joked. "We've made arrangements to have the site guarded around the clock, though, so everything should be safe."

"Do you think you'll find more of the baron's treasure?" asked Neil.

"Maybe," said the professor. "We'll certainly look hard for it — now that we know where to look." She took the bone out of the box on the table and passed it around so they could all take a look.

"It's beautiful," said Carole Parker. "It looks as if there's something carved on it here. Letters, perhaps. Any idea what it is?"

The professor shook her head. "We've taken a rubbing and sent it to a specialist in medieval languages. I'll let you know what he says."

Carole returned the bone to Professor Tate.

"Now, there's just one more thing I want to say before Jake starts his interviews," the professor continued. "Because the bone is very special to Padsham, the museum trustees are interested in buying it. Once it's been properly valued and declared an artifact, they'll offer a substantial sum to the person who actually found the bone."

The professor smiled at Neil and Emily and they, in turn, stared at Sarah. Their little sister looked thoughtful. Finally, she said in a small voice, "I didn't find the bone; Digger did. Mr. Hamley pulled me out of the hole and then we found Digger, and he'd dug up the bone."

"But isn't Digger your dog?" The professor looked confused.

"No," Neil replied. "We only own Jake, the Border collie you met yesterday. We're just walking Digger for his owners, the Thomsons. They're the ones who should get the money for the bone, if it *does* turn out to be gold."

"Neil's right," Carole said. "We must tell Mr. and Mrs. Thomson about it."

"Here's my telephone number. Ask them to call me, so we can discuss it," said Vicki Tate.

"I'd like their number, too, so I can interview them," said Jake, switching off his tape recorder. "Now, would you mind if we went to the spot where the bone was found? I'd like to take some pictures at the site."

They got the dogs and thanked Maggie Jones for looking after them. Digger licked Sarah's ankle and gazed up at her hopefully. "Come on," she said, and took off at a run with the pup bounding after her.

"You must be disappointed that the money will go to Digger's owners," Jake said to Neil as they walked down the hill together.

"A bit. We're saving up for our parents' birthday

present," Neil said quietly so that his mom wouldn't hear. "But it's only fair that the Thomsons should get it."

"Do they know about the bone yet?" asked Jake.

"They know that Digger dug something up. I told them yesterday when we took him back. But I didn't tell them that it might be a valuable artifact," said Neil.

"This is going to make a great story!" Jake said enthusiastically. "I'd like to get it in this Friday's issue, so I'll call them this evening and arrange to interview them."

"Don't tell them over the phone that the bone is made of gold — wait till you see them. Can Emily and I come with you when you go over there?" asked Neil eagerly. "I can't *wait* to see their faces when they hear what Digger found."

CHAPTER FOUR

Neil and Emily set out for the Thomsons' house later that evening, with Jake running alongside Neil's bike.

The Border collie seemed tireless. He'd already had two long walks that day, and his energy was showing no signs of flagging.

Neil spotted Jake Fielding's car already parked outside the Thomsons' gate when they arrived. As they leaned their bikes under the front window, Mr. Thomson opened the door. He was still wearing his suit and looked kind of tired, Neil thought, but he smiled as he invited them in.

"You've shampooed Digger," Neil observed, noting how clean and sleek the pup looked, perched on the sofa between Liam and Fiona.

"Well, he certainly needed a wash after yesterday's escapade," laughed Mrs. Thomson. "Now, what exactly is all the fuss about? Jake won't say a word. He wanted you to break the good news to us — whatever it is!"

Neil glanced at the reporter, then cleared his throat importantly. "We met Professor Tate this morning," he told everyone. "She says the bone Digger dug up yesterday is probably made of gold, and Padsham Castle Museum wants to buy it. Digger was the one who found it, so that means the golden bone belongs to you!"

"Wow!" cried Liam.

"That means we can get a computer!" said Fiona. Jake took a photo of her and, as his flashbulb went off, Digger barked and jumped up. He ran around the room, trying to trip everyone up, and Jake scrambled after him.

Liam grabbed Digger's collar. "Sit," he said firmly, but the puppy jumped onto his lap instead.

"That's fantastic news," said Mr. Thomson. "A little extra money is always useful. It might help with the extension we're planning. Now that the children are getting bigger, we could use the extra space."

"Digger could use it, too!" Mrs. Thomson joked.

"I wouldn't bank on it being worth *that* much, but you never know," Neil said. "Professor Tate says she'll contact you as soon as it's been properly valued."

"Well, the money's not important, really," said Mrs. Thomson. "We're just proud of what a clever dog we've got!"

Jake took a few more photographs, asked them all some questions, and then left, telling them to expect to see themselves on the front page of the *Compton News* on Friday. It was Wednesday, so they only had two days to wait.

"Thanks for walking Digger for us," Mr. Thomson said as Neil and Emily got up to go. "He was a bit hyperactive before, but he's settling down now with all the exercise."

He picked the pup up and stroked his muzzle gently, then scratched him under the chin. Digger's eyes closed in bliss. *There's a real bond between them. Those two adore each other,* thought Neil. They couldn't have found a better family to adopt Digger.

"We'd love to come and visit you soon, and see the kennel," Liam said longingly as Neil and Emily were leaving.

"Why don't you come tomorrow, and bring Digger?" Emily suggested.

"That would be great!" said Fiona, looking questioningly at her mom and dad.

"We'd be happy to show you around," offered Neil.

Mrs. Thomson smiled. "Of course you can go," she said. "It'll give me some time alone!"

* * *

The next morning, while Emily and Sarah showed Liam and Fiona around King Street Kennels, Neil biked over to Mrs. Mitchell's house with Jake, to walk Banana as promised. The dachshund pricked up her ears and wagged her thin, pointy tail when she saw Neil and Jake.

"I hope my girl's behaving herself," Mrs. Mitchell said.

Neil took his chance to broach the subject of Banana's apparent laziness. "Well, the trouble is, she keeps sitting down and not wanting to walk. I was wondering whether she had any joint problems."

Mrs. Mitchell shrugged. "Not to my knowledge," she replied vaguely. "I'm sorry she's giving you trouble. I think she's just lazy. It's hot and she's not used to so much exercise."

"How old is she?" asked Neil.

"I've had her a year. She belonged to a neighbor of my brother's, who was moving abroad. He said she was about eight," Mrs. Mitchell said.

"Dachshunds can live to fourteen or so, so she's only middle-aged," Neil said.

"So am I, and I don't like running around on hot days, either!" laughed Mrs. Mitchell.

"I still don't think it would hurt to ask the vet to check her, next time you're taking her in for anything," Neil said.

"Oh, I'm sure it won't be necessary," said Mrs. Mitchell dismissively.

But Neil wasn't so sure. He took the dachshund for a gentle stroll in a small park near her home. Again, Banana insisted on walking slowly, and Neil could tell how frustrated Jake was by the pace. The Border collie kept jumping up at Neil impatiently, then racing around him in circles.

Mrs. Mitchell was out when Neil returned. She had given Neil her spare key, so he let Banana in, got his bike from the front hall, then set off with Jake toward the site of the hole. He was dying to see if Professor Tate had unearthed anything else.

When they'd left the site the previous day, some men from the council had just arrived and were putting up a fence and a sign that read: DANGER! KEEP OUT! Now, the area was a hive of activity. A security guard with a walkie-talkie was parading the area, two large white vans were parked on the rough ground, and people were staggering around with big lights and cables. *It looks as if Professor Tate is planning an all-night dig*, thought Neil.

He couldn't see the professor, so he decided to go up to the castle to check if she was working at her original site. As he biked slowly up the steep road, a red sports car overtook him, its tires crunching on the gravel surface. The tailwind caused his bike to wobble so that he almost steered into Jake, who was trotting alongside his front wheel. He wrenched the handlebars in the opposite direction, the bike lurched to a sudden halt, and he fell off.

"Road hog!" he yelled after the offending vehicle.

Before he could get up, Jake bounded over and covered Neil's face with anxious licks, relieved to find that his best friend was OK.

"Silly dog!" Neil gave the young collie an affection-ate hug and a rub, then got up and dusted himself off.

Feeling slightly shaken, he pushed his bike the rest of the way up to the castle. The red car had stopped in the parking lot and a dark-haired man with a mustache was helping a woman out of it. Neil stopped and stared. She looked like a movie star, with her sun-bronzed skin, shiny blond hair, and clingy white dress. She looked strangely familiar, but Neil couldn't place her.

Jake pawed his leg, anxious to move on. "Come on, boy, let's see if we can find the professor," he said.

There was no sign of Professor Tate, but Mr. Hamley was down in a trench, looking hot and sunburned as he scraped away at the soil with a small trowel.

"Hello, Mr. Hamley! How's it going?" Neil called down to him. It was strange to see his teacher so casually dressed and dirty-looking!

"Fine, thanks," Mr. Hamley called back. "Heard about the TV show, Neil?"

"No. What TV show?" Neil shouted down at him.

"Hang on a minute." Mr. Hamley clambered out of the trench and walked over to him. He patted Jake, then took off his steamy glasses, polished them on his handkerchief, and popped them back on his perspiring nose. "There. I can see you now," he said.

He told Neil that some months ago, researchers for a new archaeology series had contacted Professor Tate to see if she was working on anything they might be interested in filming. "The series investigates myths and legends to see if there's any historical basis for them," he explained. "There are lots of myths associated with the ancient Padsham Castle, and since Professor Tate is in the process of uncovering its foundation, she's perfect for the series. They want to film her and her team at work, and interview her, of course."

"So that's what the lights and cables are for!" Neil exclaimed. "I don't understand, though. If they're going to film her digging up the foundations, what are they doing at Digger's treasure site?"

"What do you think?" Mr. Hamley grinned. "The show's director thinks the story of the baron's treasure is much more exciting than the old foundations of the castle."

"Well, it is," Neil agreed.

"And there's something else. I heard them talking about wanting you, Emily, Sarah — and Digger, of course — to appear on the show, too," said Mr. Hamley.

"That would be fantastic!" Neil grinned.

"I'm sure Professor Tate will be in touch with you later today," said Mr. Hamley.

"Cool!" said Neil, getting on his bike. He couldn't wait to tell Emily and Sarah!

CHAPTER FIVE

"**H**ere it is," said Bob Parker with a grin the next day, slapping four copies of the *Compton News* down on the kitchen table. Neil and Emily had rushed back from exercising Banana and Digger to see their story in the paper.

"Ooh, look at Digger! Doesn't he look sweet?" Sarah sighed. Everyone agreed. The portrait of the pup, with his head cocked to one side and his tongue hanging out, was so appealing that you wanted to pick him right off the page and cuddle him.

DIGGER'S TREASURE! PUPPY PATROL STRIKES GOLD, read the headline.

The article told the story of how Digger had discovered the golden bone while the Parker children were walking him for his owners, the Thomson family. There was a smaller picture of Digger with Liam and Fiona, and one of Neil, Emily, and Sarah. The article mentioned that Digger was the rightful owner of the bone and that once it had been valued, the Thomsons could receive a substantial reward.

We're sure that Neil, Emily, and Sarah will be rewarded, too, for if they hadn't been in the right place at the right time, the valuable relic might have remained hidden forever, the article concluded.

"Do you think they really *will* share any of it with us?" Emily asked hopefully. She was looking at Neil as she said it. He knew what she was thinking. *The birthday present fund!*

Just then the local vet, Mike Turner, called, wanting to know more about the treasure story. Neil took the opportunity to tell him about Banana.

"She's not one of my patients. I'd certainly remember a dachshund called Banana!" Mike chuckled. "But tell her owner to get the dog checked. It could be a back or a hip problem. Dachshunds are prone to them, because they have such long backs. Things can easily go out of joint, especially when the dogs are climbing stairs."

I really must persuade Mrs. Mitchell to get Banana checked out, Neil thought as he hung up the phone.

"It's not fair!" Sarah moaned. "I want to see Digger *every* day!"

"Liam and Fiona want to spend some time with him, too," Bob reminded her cheerfully. "He's their puppy, after all!"

It was a Saturday, so neither the Thomsons nor Mrs. Mitchell needed them to do any dog-walking. Bob, Neil, Emily, and Sarah were on their way back from visiting Carole Parker's brother, Jack Tansley. Neil had been happy to go along. It had been some time since he had seen their cousin Steve, and Ricky, the Tansleys' disobedient but lovable golden Labrador.

As they approached the gates of King Street Kennels, they heard an enormous racket. It sounded as if every dog in the kennel blocks and rescue center was barking at the same time. From the back of the car, Jake added his excited voice to the pandemonium. Mingled with the barks, Neil's sharp ears caught the sound of raised, arguing human voices.

Bob turned the Range Rover into the courtyard, where a large silver Volvo was parked. Now Neil could see where the voices were coming from. A well-dressed man and woman, with a little girl, were confronting his mother, while Kate and Bev, King Street Kennels' two full-time kennel assistants, hovered nearby.

"This looks like trouble . . ." said Neil, quickly undoing his seat belt.

"That man's shouting at Mommy!" Sarah cried.

"Hang on, Neil. Let me go and see what's happening first," Bob said, baffled. "Stay here while I find out."

"Where's the dog?" Neil heard the gray-haired man demand. "You must know where he is — your children were with him when he found the treasure!"

"It's about Digger! I'm getting out," Neil said urgently.

"So am I. Come on, Sarah," said Emily. Letting Jake out of the back, they went over to join the group. Jake immediately ran over to the little girl, who screamed and jumped away when he sniffed her.

"Come here, Jake," Neil ordered his boisterous dog.

Carole looked relieved to see her husband. "Bob, these people think they own Digger," she explained.

"We *do* own him! And we want the address of these Thomson people who are claiming that the dog belongs to them." The man waved a copy of the *Compton News*. "We saw the item about the treasure on the local TV news this morning. They showed a picture of the dog and, as soon as we saw him, we knew it was our missing Tinker! We've driven all the way from Liverpool to get him back."

"But how did you know to come here?" Neil asked them.

"Because it said that the three children who were

with the dog when he found the golden bone were from King Street Kennels in Compton," said the woman. "We tried to get the Thomsons' address first from the *Compton News*, but they wouldn't give it out. So we came straight here, hoping you could help us." She had a soft voice with a Scottish accent and was younger and looked friendlier than her husband.

"Would you mind telling me who you are?" Bob inquired frostily. "We can't have people just showing up here claiming to own a dog. What proof of identity do you have?"

"Our name's Carter," the woman informed him. "Tinker was Isobel's puppy. You were very upset when we lost him, weren't you, Isobel?" She looked down at her daughter, but the little girl just turned away, a sulky expression on her face as she swung one foot and tugged at her mother's hand. She didn't seem to show a spark of interest in being reunited with her puppy — *if he* was *hers,* thought Neil.

"Just tell us where the Thomsons live, so we can go and get him back," insisted Mr. Carter.

"I'm afraid I can't do that," said Bob calmly.

"Well, we're not leaving without our pup. Are we, Isobel?"

"No, Daddy," the little girl replied.

Something's definitely wrong, thought Neil. If Isobel really loved Tinker, then surely she'd be pleading with her parents to take her straight to him. He could just imagine the fuss that Sarah would have made in similar circumstances! But the sullen little girl, with her fluffy blond hair, was acting as if she couldn't care less.

"Then I'll go and call the Thomsons and ask them to come down here. I think it's better if we all discuss this on neutral territory," Bob said sensibly.

While Bob went to the office to call the Thomsons,

Carole took a tearful Sarah indoors. Bev and Kate went to look after a German shepherd who had just arrived for a two-week stay at the boarding kennel, leaving Neil and Emily alone with the Carters.

Emily smiled at Isobel. "Would you like to see the kennel and meet some of our dogs?" she invited. "You can pet Jake if you like."

But Isobel shook her head and ignored the Border collie, who was sitting in front of her and wagging his tail. Even her parents didn't seem at all interested in being shown around. Emily looked at Neil and shrugged. He could tell that, like him, she thought their behavior was very strange indeed. Any normal dog-lover would have jumped at the opportunity. And if the Carters weren't interested in dogs, it wasn't difficult to figure out what they *were* interested in . . .

Bob soon reappeared, looking grim.

"Were they in?" Neil asked him.

"Yes, they were — and they're very upset." Bob looked at Mr. Carter sternly. "Let me tell you about Digger and the Thomsons," he said. "Digger was a very cold, hungry, and frightened pup when we found him. We took him into our rescue center and nursed him back to health."

"We did everything we possibly could to find his owners," added Neil, "and when they didn't come forward, the Thomsons adopted him —"

"They had no right," Mr. Carter interrupted.

Bob glared at him. "The children, Liam and Fiona, adore him. Not only is he loved by everyone in the family, he's extremely well cared for. Unless you can offer him similar love and commitment, I would strongly oppose any efforts on your behalf to take him away from them," he said.

Neil was relieved when Mr. Thomson's old car pulled up. But he and Liam had hardly climbed out of the car when Mr. Carter demanded, "Where's my dog?"

"We left Digger at home with my wife and daughter. My little girl's very upset," Mr. Thomson replied stiffly.

"So's mine," Mr. Carter responded. "I suggest you go and get him right now. He's our dog!"

"No, he's not," Mr. Thomson insisted.

Mr. Carter rolled up his sleeves, as if preparing for a fight, but Bob Parker stepped between the two angry men. "Calm down, Mr. Carter. Losing your temper won't solve anything," he said. "Let's try to work this out like civilized human beings."

"All we want is our dog back," said Mr. Carter stubbornly.

"He's Isobel's dog," Mrs. Carter broke in. "My mother bought him," she explained. "The pup was a present for Isobel's seventh birthday."

"Yes. What *was* that woman thinking of, buying our girl a dog just when we were about to move?" Mr.

Carter glared at his wife. Neil guessed this was a long-standing family argument.

"How exactly did you lose him?" asked Carole.

"It happened the day we were moving from Kent to Liverpool," Mrs. Carter explained, giving the date. "There'd been an accident on the freeway, so we took a cross-country route instead. We let Tinker out to stretch his legs, but something frightened him and he ran away."

"We couldn't spend much time looking for him because we were in the middle of moving to a new house," Mr. Carter added. "We had more pressing matters to deal with."

"'More pressing matters'? So you just abandoned him?" Mr. Thomson asked incredulously. "A tiny puppy?"

Mr. Carter shrugged. "What else could we do? We had to get to Liverpool and pick up the key to our new home."

"A few days later, after we'd unpacked and settled in, we did make attempts to find him," Mrs. Carter said.

"What kind of attempts?" Neil asked suspiciously. His father glanced at him, as if warning him not to go too far. He knew how quickly Neil's temper flared if he suspected someone had mistreated or abandoned a dog.

"We called Battersea Dogs' Home. We thought that

was where all stray dogs were taken. We don't know much about dogs, you see," Mr. Carter explained.

Neil tried not to laugh. How could he have possibly thought that a dog that went missing in Compton could end up two hundred miles away, in London?

"Didn't you think of contacting the police, or the SPCA?" he asked.

"We did call the Liverpool police, but they said there wasn't much they could do," Mrs. Carter said.

Neil exchanged glances with his dad. Did these people live in a parallel universe, or were they just completely lacking in common sense? "You didn't think of calling the police in the Compton area?" he said.

Mrs. Carter shrugged and looked sheepish. "I had no clue where we were when we lost Tinker. I didn't even know Compton existed!" she explained.

Neil frowned. It was no excuse. The Carters obviously hadn't made a real effort to find Digger, and there was only one reason why they would want him back now. If they could claim they were Digger's owners, then the golden bone would belong to them.

"So you didn't see Digger again till you saw his picture on TV?" Bob Parker probed.

"That's right," Mr. Carter confirmed. "We recognized him immediately. He's our Tinker, all right. He's got the same markings on his face — I'd know them anywhere."

"But there could be lots of similar puppies," Liam pointed out. "How do you know it's him?"

"Tinker had distinctive orange splotches by his eyes, like little eyebrows," said Mrs. Carter.

Neil's heart sank. Digger had those features, too.

Emily had been quiet all this time, listening to the exchange. Now, she stepped in. "Have you got any real proof that Digger's yours?" she asked.

Mrs. Carter rummaged in her large black shoulder bag. She pulled out a photograph and handed it to Emily. "Here you are," she said.

Emily glanced at it and passed it to Neil. There was no doubt at all that the puppy sitting on Isobel's lap and gazing soulfully at the camera was Digger.

"And here's the receipt from the pet shop where my mother-in-law bought Tinker," said Mr. Carter, taking a folded piece of paper out of his wallet. "You can keep this — it's a photocopy. I've got the original at home."

"Receipts can easily be forged," said Mr. Thomson suspiciously.

Mr. Carter drew himself up to his full height. "If you're accusing me —" he began, raising his voice.

"Please, Brian," said Mrs. Carter, seizing her husband's arm.

Mr. Carter took a deep breath and cleared his throat. "Enough. I believe I've shown you all the evi-

dence now," he said. "Why don't you just hand the
dog over so we can leave in peace?"

Mr. Carter had obviously intended to have the last
word, but Isobel thought otherwise. To Neil's amaze-
ment, the girl burst into tears, flew at her father, and
cried, "I don't want Tinker back. I *hate* him! He's horrible, and he'll frighten Princess Melinda."

CHAPTER SIX

"**W**ho's Princess Melinda?" Neil asked the Carters' daughter.

Isobel smiled for the first time. "She's my kitty," she replied. "She's white and very soft and furry. She hates dogs — and so do I!"

Mr. Carter glared at his daughter. Mrs. Carter put a protective arm around her.

At last, her behavior made sense to Neil. No wonder she didn't want to have Digger back. If Isobel loved cats and was scared of dogs, then surely Mr. and Mrs. Carter would have more sense than to inflict Digger on her and make both daughter and dog very unhappy? Were they really that greedy for money?

"I know you love Princess Melinda, Isobel," said

her mother, "but why not just meet Tinker again? You might like him, too."

"I've got no objection to you seeing him," said Mr. Thomson. "In fact, I'm quite willing to go and get him. But I won't hear of you taking him with you until we've properly worked out this ownership business."

"I'll call the shop, if you like," Carole offered. "What's your mother's name, Mrs. Carter?"

"Smith," Isobel's mother supplied. "The pet shop will have records of all their sales."

"OK," said Carole. She disappeared into the office. There was an uncomfortable silence. Mr. Carter stood frowning, with his arms folded. *He doesn't look like he's going to give up on Digger,* thought Neil.

Shortly afterward, Carole returned. She looked surprisingly cheerful. "They say they're too busy to check right now. They've asked me to call back on Monday," she said brightly. "So, I think it's probably best if we wait till then to resolve the situation. If you'll excuse me, I have to go and check on Sarah," she added, going back inside.

Mr. Carter looked furious. His wife quickly took his arm. "Mrs. Parker's right. Come on, let's go now," she suggested. "It's a long drive home and Isobel's very tired. We know where Tinker is, so let's sort it all out next week."

Reluctantly, Mr. Carter agreed. As the Carters got

into the Volvo, Mr. Thomson thanked Bob for his help, and he and Liam headed for home, too. Liam looked thoroughly miserable.

"What do you think their chances are of keeping him?" Neil asked his father.

Bob shrugged. "It all depends," he replied. "If the shop verifies the sale to Mrs. Smith, then the Carters have the legal right to take Digger back."

"Oh, *no,*" Emily groaned.

"Even though Isobel hates him?" asked Neil, appalled.

"I'm afraid so. If it came to a legal dispute, I think the court would agree that the puppy was theirs to start with," Bob said.

"But surely we can prove that they abandoned him," said Neil. "I bet they're only after the money from the golden bone. It's so obvious. Why else would they want Digger back now?" said Neil.

"You may be right, Neil, but that would be very hard to prove," said Bob. "All we can hope is that the Carters come to their senses and allow Isobel to keep her cat and the Thomsons to keep Digger."

"Good news!" called Carole, poking her head out the kitchen door. "That was someone from the *Living Legends* production office on the phone. They'd like to meet you, Liam, and Fiona by the gates of Padsham Castle at midday tomorrow. They want to interview all of you for the TV program!"

Emily frowned. "What about Digger?" she asked.

Carole burst out laughing. "Of course they want Digger," she said. "He's the most important of all!"

The following morning the Parkers found Liam, Fiona, and Digger waiting for them at the castle entrance. As they all headed for the castle, a tousled, grubby figure came racing toward them from the direction of the museum, auburn hair flying.

"I'm so glad I caught you first," Vicki Tate panted, sounding quite distracted. "It's all Mr. Jepson's fault, the horrible man! He's way too full of himself. And that Mrs. Jepson! What a vain woman! She —"

"Slow down, Vicki," Carole Parker said, taking the emotional professor's arm. "We don't know what you're talking about. Why don't you take a deep breath, then try to tell us exactly what happened?" she suggested.

"I'm sorry. It was just such a shock!" Vicki Tate blinked her vivid blue eyes and looked a bit tearful as she explained. "Councillor Jepson has just given his permission for the *Living Legends'* archaeologist to dig up the treasure site instead of me."

"But why?" Neil asked, perplexed. "I thought you already had permission to dig here."

"Within the castle grounds, yes. But the treasure site is outside, and that land belongs to the council. Anyone can apply to dig there. It looks like the TV people bribed Mr. Jepson by telling him that he and his wife could appear on TV," the professor explained. "I'm furious!"

"But you're the local archaeologist, and you're the one who's been working on this dig," Carole pointed out. "Surely they need you and your knowledge?"

Professor Tate shrugged. "They don't need me. They don't even want to interview me now — the archaeologist who hosts the *Living Legends* series has taken over everything. They're hoping to turn her into a television superstar. You've probably heard of her. Professor Herbert!" Vicki Tate gave a shudder.

"Not the same Professor Herbert who writes those glossy books on the Pyramids and ancient Greece? I've got one of her books at home," said Emily.

"The very same," Professor Tate replied.

Suddenly, Neil realized that the glamorous blond woman who had nearly knocked him off his bike must be Professor Herbert. She had looked familiar because he had seen her on the back cover of Emily's book!

"We went to college together," the professor went on, "but I became an academic, while she took the popular route and decided to write books and get into television. She's not the type who'd stand up to her knees in dirt in a trench. She never could stand getting her fingernails dirty."

She glanced down at her own and grimaced.

"But you've worked so hard on this dig," said Neil.

"I know," said Vicki Tate. "I've devoted the last six months to it. A couple of my students are even basing their theses on it. But now that *she's* involved, everything will be ruined. If she finds any treasure, you can bet she'll bask in the fame and glory, whereas I just want the credit for my university."

"That's terrible," said Carole sympathetically.

"I don't want to take part in the program now," Emily added.

"Neither do we," said Liam forcefully.

Just then, Neil saw a familiar red car pull up nearby. Gliding toward them in a glamorous black dress and a pair of high-heeled sandals was the glossy blond woman whose car had nearly knocked Neil off his bike. She was holding the golden bone between her finger and thumb, as if she was afraid there might still be some dirt clinging to it.

"Oh, there you all are," she said with a beaming smile. "And this must be the famous Digger." Neil noticed that she made no move to pat Digger. In fact, when the puppy heard his name and took a step toward her, Professor Herbert immediately stepped back.

"Don't hold the bone like that, Helen!" snapped Vicki Tate.

"I'm aware of its value, Vicki," Helen Herbert said coolly.

"And *I'm* aware of how you flattered Councillor

Jepson in order to get your own way on the dig!"
Vicki responded.

Professor Herbert looked amused. "You and I go
back a long way, Vicki. I know we've both done different things, but we're both professionals. I've got
my methods, you've got yours."

She seemed totally cold and in control. Neil dis-
liked her more and more.

"So let's get started, shall we?" Professor Herbert
said. "I'd like to record the story of how you kids and
Digger found the treasure, then I'll date and identify
the bone for the records."

"Don't you dare!" Professor Tate stepped up close

to her rival. "There hasn't even been time to get the bone valued yet. It's my responsibility. You may have the permission to dig for further artifacts, but this one's mine and *I'm* going to tell your viewers about it. Hand the bone over — now!"

Helen Herbert hesitated, and in that split second, Digger intervened. Jerking his leash out of Fiona's hand, he made a jump, snatched the golden bone from Professor Herbert's fingers, and set off at full speed across the lawn.

"Digger! Come here!" cried Liam.

Neil's reactions were the quickest. He raced after Digger, calling his name. Digger glanced back, saw Neil following him, and darted into some bushes near the tall stone wall of the castle grounds. Neil had almost caught up with him when he stubbed his foot against a stone that was hidden in the undergrowth.

As he went sprawling, he caught a brief glimpse of what Digger was up to. The puppy's paws were flying as he dug a hole underneath a thick holly bush. By the time Neil was back on his feet, Digger had reappeared. He was wagging his tail happily, but the bone was nowhere to be seen.

Neil was just about to look for the bone when he suddenly had second thoughts and stopped. If everyone believed the bone was lost, the two professors would stop arguing. And, more important, the Carters might go away and leave Digger and the Thomsons in peace. He was convinced they were only after Digger for the money.

Taking Digger's leash, he took a long route around the bushes and reappeared just as Professor Tate was approaching. Hot on her heels were his mother and sisters, followed by Liam and Fiona. Farther up the path, he could see Professor Herbert making slow progress on the rough ground in her high-heeled sandals.

"Where's the bone?" Vicki Tate panted.

Neil shrugged. "I don't know. Digger must have dropped it somewhere."

"But you *must* know!" she insisted. "You were right behind him. Didn't you see anything?"

"Come on, Neil," urged his mother.

Neil saw Emily looking at him quizzically. He tried not to give anything away and stuck firmly to his story.

Professor Herbert arrived at last. Her tanned face went a shade paler when Neil repeated to her that Digger had lost the bone. "I don't believe you," she said. "Pull out your pockets!"

Neil promptly did as he was asked, proving that he didn't have the golden bone on him. But Professor Herbert still wasn't satisfied, and even Professor Tate was staring at him suspiciously.

"By the time I found Digger, he'd dropped it somewhere," Neil insisted.

"I think you're lying," snapped Professor Herbert,

fixing him with an icy stare. "This is a setup! You and Vicki planned it to make a fool of me. Well, I'm on to your little game. If you think you're going to get that bone the minute my back's turned, and then give it back to Vicki Tate, you've got another thing coming, Neil Parker. Find it this minute!"

Carole Parker stepped forward. "Look, I realize you're upset, but I don't think you've got the right to accuse Neil of lying," she said.

"Digger can be a bit naughty sometimes," added Liam. "He's always burying things in our garden. Money, shoes, even Dad's reading glasses."

"Well, I'll just have to find the bone myself, won't I? You all might as well go now," she told the Parkers and the Thomsons. "If there's no bone, there's no story."

"This is terrible!" Professor Tate looked close to tears. "Are you *sure* you have no idea where it is, Neil?"

Neil shook his head and shrugged apologetically. He liked Vicki Tate and felt guilty about lying to her, but he was sure he'd done the right thing, and for the right reason.

Back at King Street Kennels, Neil told Emily his secret and made her promise not to tell a soul. At first she was shocked that Neil had lied in front of so many people.

"Aren't you at least going to tell Professor Tate the truth?" she asked.

"Think about it, Em," said Neil. "If the Carters are only after the money, they'll give up their claim on Digger when they hear that the bone's lost."

"Of course!" said Emily.

"I feel bad about lying to Professor Tate, but I just *had* to. I did it for Digger."

CHAPTER SEVEN

"**K**ing Street Kennels. May I help you?" asked Neil, struggling with a huge bag of dog biscuits as he balanced the telephone receiver under his chin.

"Mr. Parker?" a voice inquired.

"No, it's —"

The woman at the other end of the phone didn't wait for Neil to explain who he was. "We've found it for you," she continued. "One black-and-tan mongrel puppy, with vaccination certificates, sold to a Mrs. Smith." She told him the date and mentioned the other items Mrs. Smith had bought — puppy food, a collar, a bed, and a carrying case. "Is that the information you wanted?" she asked.

"Yes. Thank you," Neil replied.

He replaced the receiver and chewed his lower lip

thoughtfully. So the Carters' story was true, after all. Isobel's grandma really *had* bought Digger for her. The dates checked out, too. The pup had been bought just three days before the Carters' departure, and had been missing for four days when Neil and Sarah rescued him.

Nothing made Neil more angry than irresponsible people who got dogs. Isobel's grandmother must have known the family was about to move to Liverpool. It was the worst possible time to buy Isobel a dog, as Mr. Carter had pointed out. Not only that, she'd obviously done it without asking if Isobel even wanted one!

Neil felt sorry for Isobel Carter. He knew some people didn't like dogs, though he couldn't possibly imagine why. As far as he was concerned, nothing in the universe was better than a puppy. And Digger was one of the most friendly, spirited, and intelligent puppies he had ever met.

He took the bag of dog biscuits out to Kate in Kennel Block One and went to find his mother in the office. When he told her the news, she said, "Well, even though the Carters' claim has been backed up, I don't think it will matter now, as long as the bone doesn't turn up. They could have found Digger when he was first lost if they'd tried hard enough — it obviously has to do with the reward."

The whole Parker family had cheered up at the news that Digger had reburied the golden bone. Neil was determined not to tell anyone else that he knew where it was.

"Has anyone told the Carters it's lost yet?" Neil inquired.

"No. I think we should wait a little while in case one of the professors finds it," his mother said sensibly. She paused, then added, "I really do hope the bone doesn't turn up, though. It will save everyone a lot of stress."

"You bet!" Neil replied, hoping his face wasn't giving away any trace of the guilt that he felt.

The weather had broken in the night and, although the rain had eased off by the middle of the morning, it was still drizzling. But Digger and Banana needed walking all the same.

"How much money have we earned so far?" Emily asked her brother as they biked toward Padsham that afternoon, dressed in raincoats and boots.

"Not enough. We're still only halfway there," Neil replied.

"Do you think we'll make it in time? Don't forget that we'll have to order the photograph, and that could take a few days . . ."

"I've already checked that out. They estimate they can turn around our order in three days — two if we can pick up the photo ourselves," Neil said. "It's Monday today, and we've got until a week from Friday."

"So we might still do it," said Emily.

"Hope so," said Neil, crossing his fingers. "Come on, Jake!" The young Border collie left his investigations of a lamppost and trotted along the pavement beside Neil's bike.

As they were wheeling their bikes onto the Thomson's porch, Digger raced into the front yard, barking like crazy. A streak of ginger fur shot out from under a hydrangea bush and disappeared through a hole in the next-door neighbor's garden fence. Digger pushed his nose through the hole and kept on barking.

"He's a cat hunter, that one," said Mrs. Thomson. "Won't leave them alone. I think he'd eat them, given half a chance. Come here, you bad dog!"

Mrs. Thomson clipped on Digger's leash and handed it to Neil with a relieved smile. "Have fun! I hope he's not too much of a handful," she called after them as they headed for Mrs. Mitchell's to pick up Banana.

Neil and Emily's goal for the day was to find out if Mrs. Mitchell had taken the dachshund to see a vet yet. However, to Emily's surprise, and Neil's indignation, it appeared that Banana didn't even have a regular vet. *No wonder Mrs. Mitchell seemed so vague the last time I mentioned the subject*, Neil thought.

"I've heard very good things about Mike Turner," Mrs. Mitchell said. "I don't mind at all if he takes a look at Banana. Maybe there *is* something wrong, after all. I'll just have to find the time to make an appointment."

Neil gave his sister a secret thumbs-up sign. Success!

Despite the weather, they were looking forward to walking the dogs around Padsham Castle. The rain meant that they would probably have the place to themselves. From what they'd seen of Professor Herbert, they couldn't imagine her wanting to get her hair or her feet wet!

As soon as they neared the castle gates, they let Banana off the leash, but Neil didn't dare unclip Digger until they were through the gates and well on their way up the hill. He didn't want the puppy to remember where he'd hidden the bone and dash off to dig it up again.

"I think we should steer clear of anywhere the professors might be lurking. I don't want the third degree about the bone again," said Neil firmly. He was still feeling guilty about Professor Tate and didn't want to see her unhappy face.

As they climbed higher, Padsham Castle looked magnificently spooky, its gray battlements looming up into the rain clouds. *All it needs*, thought Neil, *is a flash of lightning to transform it into the home of Count Dracula!* No one, not even Mr. Hamley, was working on the site of the Norman remains that day. The trenches and holes were covered with plastic sheeting to protect them from the rainwater.

Hearing a series of high-pitched yaps, they turned

to see Toby the terrier racing toward them. He
jumped around the other dogs, trying to persuade
them to play. Neil threw a stick, and Jake and Digger shot off like rockets. Neil and Emily laughed as
they watched the dogs racing for it.

Digger raced back to Neil with the stick in his
mouth. He gave Neil a playful look, his ears raised,
but when Neil ordered him to drop the stick he refused, and growled playfully. The result was a serious bout of tug-of-war. "Crazy pup! You need to come
to Dad's obedience classes," said Neil.

"Go on, Banana, you lazy dog," urged Emily as the
dachshund parked herself on Emily's foot. "Get off
my boot!"

"Stay here for a moment and keep your eye on the

dogs. I'm going to see if Mrs. Jones is around," said Neil. "I'm craving a mug of her hot chocolate."

It was a big mistake. No sooner had Neil passed through the entrance than he spotted Professor Herbert. She swooped on him immediately, her perfect teeth flashing a friendly smile.

"Neil Parker! The one and only!" she said. "We're waiting for the rain to stop so we can resume filming — the forecast said it'll be drier this afternoon. I knew I'd bump into you if I waited long enough. Mrs. Jones told me you've been walking the dogs here lately, around this time of the day."

Hearing her name, Mrs. Jones looked up from her ticket desk and gave him a wave. Neil groaned inwardly as he waved back. Why, oh *why*, did she have to tell Dr. Herbert that?

Even in wet weather gear, the blond archaeologist looked glamorous. She was wearing a shiny red vinyl raincoat and boots, along with dangly earrings that matched her outfit.

Expecting a grilling on the subject of the missing golden bone, Neil was pleasantly surprised when instead she said, "I've got a video I'd like you and your sister to see."

Neil frowned. "What kind of video?" he asked. Something was up, he was sure. Professor Herbert was being far too nice all of a sudden.

Helen Herbert laughed. "What kind do you think?

Archaeology, of course! *And* dogs! It's a program I made in Egypt."

"Look, it's nice of you to offer, but I'd really better go and help Emily. She's waiting outside with the dogs," said Neil, eager to escape.

But he couldn't get rid of Professor Herbert that easily. "Let's go and get her then," she said, taking hold of his elbow and marching him out.

Emily didn't seem quite so suspicious of Professor Herbert's invitation. "I don't see why not . . ." she said uncertainly, as Neil shot her a warning look. "We're doing a project on ancient Egypt at school next fall."

"But what about the dogs?" Neil said, still reluctant. "We can't leave them."

"Maggie? Since there's no one around, is it OK for them to bring the dogs in while I show them this video?" Professor Herbert asked Mrs. Jones.

Mrs. Jones gave them a cheerful wink. "Go ahead. Just this once."

Neil couldn't think of any more excuses. Professor Herbert was being so friendly that he was even beginning to wonder if he'd misjudged her.

He clipped on Digger's leash so the dog wouldn't charge around and brake anything valuable. Although they were fairly familiar with the inside of the castle, they had never been down the corridor where Professor Herbert was taking them now. She opened a door and flicked a switch, and Neil saw a flight of narrow, twisting stone steps ahead of him. They led downward, into gloom. Dim bulbs set in brackets on the wall shed an eerie light. Neil descended with Digger and Jake at his side, while Emily picked Banana up and carried her, just in case the steep steps were too much for her short legs.

Somewhere down below, Neil could hear the sound of knocking and muffled shouts. "What's all that noise?" he asked.

"Just the crew knocking some props together," said Professor Herbert. "They're trying out some light and sound effects. We're doing some filming inside the castle tomorrow and we're trying to make it seem old and creepy."

The noise was coming from the other side of a huge oak door. Its large iron hinges and enormous keyhole made Neil think of Count Dracula again. Helen Herbert reached in her pocket and produced the biggest key that Neil and Emily had ever seen.

"Here we are," she announced cheerfully, turning the key in the lock. The hinges must have been kept well oiled, because the heavy door opened easily. "It might be a bit dark in here," she warned.

It certainly was. As they stepped inside, a shadowy figure jumped out of the gloom toward them. Jake barked and Emily screamed.

"Let me out of here!" the figure cried. It was Professor Tate.

"What are *you* doing in here?" The words had scarcely left Neil's lips when Professor Herbert stepped abruptly toward the door.

"The same as you two," she said. The smile didn't leave her face, but her voice became cold as she said, "Nobody is leaving this room until one of you tells me where the golden bone is. Just to help you remember, I'm taking Digger with me!" And before Neil had a chance to react, she grabbed the puppy by the collar, dragged him out, and slammed the door behind her. They were trapped. . . .

CHAPTER EIGHT

Why didn't I move faster? Neil thought angrily. *I could have stopped her, I know I could!* It was as if his legs were paralyzed in the few brief moments it took Professor Herbert to snatch up Digger's leash and shut the door.

"Let us out, *please!*" Emily screamed. Neil kept hammering on the door even though he knew it was useless.

On the other side of the door, the perplexed puppy was barking. Jake stood on his hind legs and scratched at the door, barking back to Digger. Banana joined in, too, yapping and making little runs toward the door.

Emily turned to Neil. "You don't think she'll hurt

Digger, do you?" she asked, almost in tears at the thought.

"I'm sure she won't. He's too valuable to her. After all, he's the only one who knows where the bone is buried," said Professor Tate soothingly.

Neil ignored the meaningful look that Emily gave him. He was still determined to keep quiet about the whereabouts of the bone. "How long have you been in here?" he asked the professor.

"About an hour, I think," she replied. "Helen lured me down by saying that she wanted me to give the film crew some information about the castle. I should have known better. She thinks I'm in cahoots with you. She thinks that we all know where the bone is, and that as soon as she and the film crew leave, I'll produce it and take all the credit." She turned to Neil, a distressed look in her eyes. "Are you *sure* you don't know where it is?" she pleaded. "Because if you do, you might as well tell Professor Herbert and get us all out of this ridiculous situation."

It's my fault we're all locked up in here, Neil thought guiltily. *But I just can't tell her, not even to get us out. Digger's future is at stake. . . .*

"I really don't know," he lied, aware of Emily's eyes on him again.

"I think Professor Herbert's insane," Emily said, quickly trying to change the subject.

"I don't know about insane, but she's certainly power-crazy," Vicki Tate replied. "I think she wants the whole world to see her as the leading expert on anything archaeological. Perhaps she fears that her career will be damaged if the bone isn't found — it was in her care at the time Digger stole it and she thinks that she'll be held responsible for its loss."

"Surely she wouldn't let us *starve*?" said Emily. "And what about the dogs?"

"That's what I'm most worried about, too. I hope

Professor Herbert brings them some water, at least," Neil said, giving Jake a comforting stroke. "Mrs. Mitchell and the Thomsons will soon start wondering where Banana and Digger are, though, and they'll come and look for us," he pointed out. "And maybe Mrs. Jones will raise the alarm if she doesn't see us come out. Don't worry, Em, I'm sure we'll soon be out of here. Wherever 'here' is . . ."

"We're in the dungeons," the professor explained.

Neil looked around him. The cavernous room extended back into the shadows.

"At least it's got an electric light," remarked Emily, staring at the single bulb that hung from the high ceiling on a length of cord.

"Hey, I think I can hear someone," said Professor Tate suddenly. "Help! We're in here! Help!" she yelled.

They all smiled with relief at the sound of footsteps halting outside the door. But when they heard Digger barking, their faces fell. It was only Professor Herbert. At least they knew that Digger was all right.

"Have you decided to talk yet?" she called through the door.

They held a quick whispered conference. Should they pretend they knew where the bone was, and offer to lead her to it so that she'd let them out?

But before they could agree on a plan of action, Professor Herbert spoke again. "I see. Play it your own way." Then she laughed. "Well, maybe this will help you make up your minds."

They heard her retreating footsteps ringing on the stone floor. Digger's barks grew fainter, and Jake padded back to Neil's side. Moments later, the dungeon was plunged into total darkness.

Emily screamed loudly, and Jake and Banana barked.

"This is ridiculous. Now she's turned the electricity off!" exclaimed Professor Tate.

Neil felt the comforting weight of Jake leaning against his legs in the darkness and stroked his silky head. "Is Banana OK?" he asked Emily.

"She's right by my foot, lying down," Emily reported.

"That's good. OK, let's think. How far back does this room go? What's at the other end, Professor Tate?" asked Neil.

"Please call me Vicki, Neil," the professor insisted. "There's no door or anything, just a wall. I had an hour to explore before you came. But there is one thing . . ." The professor paused, then continued, "Archibald Quinn, the eccentric millionaire who built this place in the last century, was crazy about secret passages and trapdoors. The castle is supposed to be riddled with them. Trouble is, they're all very well hidden. If only that woman hadn't taken my trowel and my flashlight!" said the professor angrily. "She asked to borrow them just before she threw me in here!"

"Very clever," commented Neil grimly. Professor Herbert had a truly devious mind. But now was his chance to outwit her! "I think we should start looking right now," he said. "It's worth a try. We can feel our way around the walls and all over the floor. If there's any way of escape, we'll find it."

According to the glow-in-the-dark dial on Neil's watch, it took half an hour for them to explore every inch of wall within reach, without finding a thing. Then they started on the floor.

"We'd better keep whistling or humming so we don't bump into each other," Professor Tate suggested. She had already collided with Neil and stepped on Emily's toe.

The dogs were another problem. Neil was very conscious of the fact that he might accidentally step on a paw or a tail. But he knew that dogs' eyes were better adapted to seeing in the dark, so it was up to Jake and Banana to keep out of their way.

He sighed heavily. He was beginning to feel hungry. How long would they have to remain in here?

A scratching, scrabbling noise from somewhere behind them made them all jump.

"I hope it's not a rat!" exclaimed Emily.

Neil grimaced. "I'm sure Jake will soon chase it away if it is."

The scratching sound continued. It was coming from the far end of the dungeon.

"Where's Banana?" said Emily suddenly. "She was curled up next to me a moment ago."

"Banana! Here, girl," Neil called.

Nails clicked on the flagstones, and then a nose nudged Neil's ankle.

"Was it you making that noise, girl?" asked Emily.

Neil bent down and groped around in the dark for the dachshund's collar. Banana pulled away from him and he almost fell. "That's funny," he said. "It's as if she's trying to take me somewhere. What a change from us pulling her along!" he added, laughing. "Give me her leash, please, Emily."

He snapped on the leash and followed Banana. Suddenly, she stopped, stood up on her hind paws, and began scrabbling at the wall again. Neil ran his hands along Banana's body, then slid them down her front legs to her paws so that he could feel what she was scratching at.

"I think there's something here!" he exclaimed excitedly. "There's some kind of notch in the wall." He explored it with his fingers. The dungeon walls were made of large stone slabs and there was a definite indentation in the one he was touching. Banana whined and pawed at it again. There was a crunch and a creak. Neil reached in front of him. His fingers encountered nothing but empty space. It was as if an entire section of stonework had swung open!

"We did it! It looks like Banana's found a trap-door!" he shouted gleefully. "Good girl, Banana!"

"Where are you? . . . Oh, there you are." Emily's hand made contact with Neil's back.

"Well, this is definitely worth investigating," said Vicki Tate, stumbling her way toward them. "Let's just hope it takes us into a tunnel."

For once, Banana was pulling on the leash, eager to explore. Neil felt Jake brush against his legs and grabbed his collar, worried that his curious dog might get lost in the maze of tunnels.

"I'd better go first. I don't want you two hurting yourselves," Vicki insisted. "Emily, you follow me, and you bring up the rear, Neil. OK?"

"Can you take Banana's leash while I look after Jake, Em?" asked Neil.

"No problem," said Emily, shivering. "Brr, it's freezing in here!" she complained as they carefully felt their way forward in the dank darkness.

Neil was relieved to discover that Banana had indeed found a tunnel. The ground felt solid enough beneath him, and he could touch the walls on either side. Edging along in the darkness, he was glad for Jake's company, because every time Neil faltered, the Border collie's whiskery nose nudged him on.

"It's OK, boy," Neil said comfortingly to Jake as the dog gave a little whine. "I know it smells old and musty in here, but I'm sure we'll reach fresh air soon." He patted Jake's head and felt his powerful tail thump against his leg.

"Are you and Banana all right?" Neil called to Emily.

"Yeah. I think Banana could use a drink, though," she replied.

"Careful! The tunnel bends to the left here," Professor Tate warned. "Wow!" she exclaimed suddenly.

"You should see this, Neil. It's amazing!" said his sister in awed tones.

"To see *anything* would be amazing," Neil responded grumpily. He was fed up with groping along in the dark. But when he reached the bend, he, too, was amazed at what he saw. Ahead of them, the passageway was lit by an eerie blue-green glow. It came from the walls of a cave into which the tunnel led.

"Phosphorescence," Neil said knowledgeably.

"Careful, it's a bit slippery here," warned Vicki.

"Look! Is that daylight up ahead?" asked Neil suddenly. It was a dazzling patch, no bigger than a plate, but it was the most hopeful sight he'd seen all day.

As they walked through the cave, the ground sloped up gradually and the light grew stronger. They were nearly at the end of the tunnel.

"I wonder where we're going to come out," said Emily.

Suddenly, Jake gave a yap and rushed past them all to the exit, barking like crazy. He scrabbled out through the undergrowth and disappeared. In the distance, Neil heard an answering bark. It sounded like Digger.

Then, to his horror, he heard the distinctive voice of Professor Herbert shouting, "Go away!"

Neil's heart sank. They'd found the tunnel and made their escape, only to walk straight into the very person who had imprisoned them.

CHAPTER NINE

"**I**'ve got to go after Jake! I don't trust Professor Herbert as far as I can throw her!" Neil declared.

"Sshh!" hissed Vicki, clutching his arm. "We don't want her to hear us."

"She can't do much to us — she's completely outnumbered," Neil reminded her.

"But she might not be alone," insisted Professor Tate. "We're safer staying here until the coast is clear. We don't know what she's capable of right now!"

"I'm going after Jake," Neil said firmly. "I've got to make sure he's OK. She may not harm Digger if she's hoping he'll lead her to the bone, but we don't know what she might do to Jake. Come on!"

Neil struggled to remove the mud, stones, and plants that blocked the exit, and pushed his way through the tunnel mouth. Emily picked Banana up and passed her to Neil, then scrambled out herself. Vicki Tate squeezed through after them.

Neil was astonished to find that the tunnel had taken them right out of the Padsham Castle grounds to the very spot where Digger had buried the golden bone!

Fortunately, there was no sign of Professor Herbert, but they could hear her shouting anxiously and Jake and Digger barking loudly. Neil smiled. "It sounds as if Jake's giving her a hard time," he said.

"Let's see what's going on," Emily urged.

"Well, it doesn't look as if Helen's in any position to play tricks on us now," said Vicki. "But let's try and stay hidden until we can see what's going on, just in case."

They crept in the direction of the barking. "Get down! Go home!" they heard Professor Herbert yell. Neil grinned at Emily. He'd been right in thinking that their captor didn't know how to handle dogs. If she was scared, the dogs would sense her fear and refuse to obey her.

"Good dog, Digger. Good boy. You — whatever your name is — *go away*. You're a nuisance!" Helen Herbert's voice was almost hysterical.

"Way to go, Jake!" muttered Neil. He guessed that the collie was playfully jumping up at her. Then he heard a menacing growl.

"Get off, get *off*!" screamed Professor Herbert. "Help, someone. *Help!*"

Neil burst out of the bushes and ran in the direction of the commotion. He found Helen Herbert with her back against the wall of the castle grounds, pinned there by Jake, who was standing on his hind legs. Jake was normally so friendly. *Where was Digger?* Neil wondered.

Helen Herbert's face was pale and she was trembling visibly. "I don't know how you escaped, but please get your dog away from me. He's terrifying me," she admitted weakly.

Neil was about to call Jake off when he had second thoughts. Standing with his arms folded, he decided to enjoy this moment of triumph for a little longer. Emily, Banana, and Professor Tate stepped up alongside him.

"I'll call off my dog on one condition," Neil said firmly. "You must give Professor Tate the right to dig where the bone was found. If she finds anything, she gets the credit."

Before Dr. Herbert could reply, Jake pushed her with his front paws. She staggered and screamed, "He's going to bite me!"

Neil knew that Jake was very unlikely to bite unless someone attacked or hurt him. Even though he was still a young dog, Jake had already received a lot of training from Neil and his father. But Neil wasn't going to tell Professor Herbert that. . . .

"We won't report you for locking us in the dungeon if you'll leave Professor Tate and the treasure alone. OK?" he asserted.

"OK," Dr. Herbert agreed weakly. "Now please, Neil . . ."

"Here, Jake," Neil called, clicking his fingers. Jake got down and ran over to Neil. *Aren't I smart?* his expression seemed to say.

"Good boy!" Neil ruffled the Border collie's black-and-white fur, and Jake wagged his tail happily.

Relieved, Helen Herbert quickly patted her hair and straightened her clothes. Vicki Tate confronted her. "I heard the agreement you and Neil made, but I'm not sure that I'm satisfied," she said. "I could have you prosecuted for the way you treated these children."

Professor Herbert bit her lip. Her face reddened.

"I'm sorry," she said. "I was desperate. I never meant to hurt anyone, but my job was on the line. I had to make a big discovery or I'd be fired — the producers said they wanted a *real* archaeologist. And I had to prove that I could do it."

"Well, tough luck!" was Professor Tate's unsympathetic reply.

Neil was only half-listening to them, he was so busy making a fuss over Jake. "Sorry, Banana. I didn't mean to leave you out," he said as the dachshund pawed his ankle and whined.

"Hey! Where's Digger?" Emily said suddenly.

"Don't ask me," said Professor Herbert in a defensive tone as they all stared at her, waiting for a response.

"Well, I wouldn't put anything past you now," said Professor Tate.

Helen Herbert opened her mouth to say something. Then she thought better of it and hurried off down the path toward her car. The car's tires dug into the gravel as it sped off down the road.

"I bet that's the last we see of *her* in Padsham," Vicki said in a satisfied tone.

There was a sudden excited yap from somewhere close by. "There's Digger! What's he up to?" Emily exclaimed.

Neil turned to see clods of wet dirt flying into the air. The next moment, the mongrel pup appeared, carrying something in his mouth.

It was the golden bone!

Digger trotted up to Neil and dropped it at his feet, wagging his tail eagerly. As Neil reached down to pat him, his heart sank. There was no time to hide the bone — the professor had already seen it.

Digger's just wrecked his whole future, Neil thought miserably as he handed the treasure to the professor. He looked down at his feet guiltily.

"Well, you don't look too surprised to see this, Neil," said Vicki, scrutinizing his face.

Neil felt himself blushing.

"You knew where it was all along, didn't you?" she said.

"Um . . ."

"Look, Neil." Vicki patted his arm. "I'm not angry with you — I just don't understand why you kept it a secret, especially when we were locked up. If you were trying to hide it from Helen, that was a kind thought, but why didn't you tell me about it? It doesn't matter now, of course, but —"

"Tell her why you did it, Neil," Emily broke in.

As Neil explained how he had been trying to protect Digger, Vicki Tate smiled sympathetically.

"I understand," she said. "Anyone who loves dogs would. You were trying to do the right thing for Digger. But I don't know what's going to happen now. You know I can't pretend that the bone's still hidden. This could be a really exciting archaeological find. There's just too much at stake. There must be *something* you can do to get rid of these Carter people. Isn't there?"

"I hope so, but I don't have a clue what," said Neil gloomily.

"We'd better be getting back," Emily said anxiously. "We've been gone for hours."

"You're right," Vicki agreed. "Your parents must be getting worried, never mind Digger's and Banana's owners."

"What are those dogs up to now?" Emily frowned. Scratching sounds were coming from the holly bush where Digger had hidden the golden bone.

"I think we'd better go and see," said Neil.

None of the dogs could be seen, but they certainly could be heard. Oddly enough, the noises seemed to be coming from the muddy ground *under* a holly bush.

"Jake! Banana! Digger! Come here," Neil called loudly.

There were muffled barks and the sound of scrabbling. Then Jake appeared, followed by Digger, with Banana waddling after them.

"What have you found *this* time?" Neil pushed a prickly holly branch aside and ducked underneath it.

"Let me see." The professor stuck her head through the holly. Under the bush was a sizable hole between two boulders, neatly excavated by the dogs.

"This could be more Norman house foundations! I'm going to get a flashlight from the security guard," Vicki Tate said.

She dashed off, returning minutes later with a large flashlight. Neil and Emily stepped aside as Professor Tate crouched down next to the hole and swept the powerful beam around. "There's something in there, all right," she said, her voice trembling with excitement. "It looks like a chest of some sort. I can't quite reach it, though."

She tutted in annoyance, then thrust in her arm as far as it would go. The torch clanged against something. "It's metal!" she said in surprise.

Jake pushed impatiently against her legs, eager to get back down the fascinating hole.

Vicki tried to squeeze her way into the hole herself, but almost got stuck in the process. She gave up in frustration. "Neil, you're smaller than me. Do you think you could crawl down there and reach the chest? Don't try to move it if it's too heavy. Just see if you can get the lid off and look inside."

Neil got down on his hands and knees in the mud. As he did so, he dislodged a shower of raindrops from a branch, and they trickled down inside the collar of his jacket. He shivered, then took the flashlight from the professor and wriggled into the hole.

The chest, blackened by dampness and time, was about eighty inches long and stood about two feet high. There was just enough headroom for Neil to crouch beside it, but when he tried to open it, he found that the hinged lid was stuck tight. Scared of damaging it, Neil worked at it gently, scraping away at the caked dirt with his fingers.

Eventually, he saw a dull gleam of silver. Then, with a protesting crack, the lid opened.

"Success!" Neil called out.

"What's inside?" gasped Vicki impatiently.

"Hang on . . ." Neil held his breath as he shined the flashlight inside. There was a red velvet bag, partly disintegrated. Sticking out of it was a large, thick ring of what seemed to be old, rotting leather. As he picked it up and examined it in the beam of the flashlight, something winked at Neil like a red eye. His pulse raced with excitement. The object looked just like a dog's collar, studded with red stones. Could they be rubies?

Keeping the flashlight as steady as he could, he reached down and pulled another object from the

bag. This time it was a small statue of a dog — possibly a wolfhound — carved from shiny black stone. Its eyes and collar were made of sparkling blue jewels.

Neil backed out of the hole, shaking with excitement. "Guess what?" he said to Emily and Professor Tate. "I think we've found the rest of the baron's treasure!"

CHAPTER TEN

"**I**'ll need to catalog everything properly and take photos before we get the chest out. This is a historic moment and it has to be recorded accurately," said Professor Vicki Tate. "It looks like the golden bone somehow got separated from the rest of the baron's treasure."

"It's a good thing we've got such smart dogs," said Neil, fondling Jake's ears.

Neil, Emily, and Vicki made their way back to the castle, excited by their find but exhausted. A group of people were gathered by the castle drawbridge, talking animatedly. As they approached, a young man with dark, curly hair detached himself from the group and came over to the professor. He introduced himself as Fitzroy Morgan, the director of *Living*

Legends. "We've just heard that Professor Herbert has resigned. That means we need another archaeologist to present the *Living Legends* series. Would you be interested in taking over for her?" he asked.

Vicki Tate's round face split into a brilliant grin. "I'd love to," she said. "In fact, if you're still interested in the story of the baron's treasure, I've got some pretty amazing news . . ."

But before she could tell anyone about finding the treasure, Mrs. Jones popped her head out of the museum doorway. "Professor Tate — telephone for you," she called.

Vicki was gone for about five minutes. She returned with an amused expression on her face. "That was my friend, the medieval languages expert, about the writing on the golden bone," she told Neil and Emily. "He says it's a crude form of Latin that, funnily enough, is known as 'Dog Latin'! The translation is, 'Dogs Are My Whole World.' Maybe it was the baron's motto."

"I think it should be Neil's motto, too," laughed Emily.

Neil and Emily left the professor deep in an excited discussion with Fitzroy Morgan. They took Banana home first, apologizing to Mrs. Mitchell for her muddy state, before delivering Digger back to the Thomsons. There were long faces all around when Mrs. Thomson, Liam, and Fiona heard that the golden bone had been found again.

"I was hoping against hope that when the Carters heard it was missing, they'd leave Digger alone, but there's no chance of that now," Mrs. Thomson said sadly. "Anyway, I wouldn't be surprised if Mr. Carter dug up all around Padsham Castle till he found it."

"What are you going to do?" asked Emily.

Mrs. Thomson shrugged hopelessly.

"Maybe you could make a deal with Mr. Carter?" suggested Neil. "Offer him half the money in exchange for Digger."

"They can have *all* the money as far as we're concerned. I don't care how much it is. No amount of money could make up for losing him." Mrs. Thomson stroked the puppy's silky ears.

"We're not giving you up, Digger," said Liam. "We're going to fight for you, boy."

"So are we," Neil assured him as they got up to go. "There's no way the Carters are going to take him away from you."

Neil and Emily said good-bye and biked home in silence. Neither of them could think of anything but the puppy's plight. Even Jake seemed subdued as he trotted alongside Neil.

"Do you think they *will* be able to keep Digger?" Emily said at last as they turned into King Street Kennels.

"If Dad can prove that the Carters aren't fit people to look after a dog, then they might be able to. But it's going to be hard work," Neil said gloomily.

As they arrived home, Bob was climbing into the Range Rover to go and look for them. "What in the world happened to you two? Look at the state you're in! *And* Jake. You all look as if you've been rolling in mud!"

"Just wait till you hear what happened," said Emily, forgetting about Digger for a moment as she remembered their exciting discovery.

"The dogs found the rest of the baron's treasure!" said Neil.

Bob raised his eyebrows. "Who needs metal detectors with dogs like Digger around!"

"And Jake. And Banana. They helped, too," said Emily. Jake gave a bark as if in agreement.

"But we've also got some bad news," said Neil. "Digger found the golden bone again — he dug it up. Professor Tate's got it. The Carters are definitely going to want Digger back now. There's no way that Mr. Carter's going to give up!"

Bob groaned. "I've already arranged for everyone to come here tonight to work out this business once and for all," he said. "I was hoping that once we told Mr. Carter the bone had gone missing he'd eventually let it go. Now it looks like we'll have a real fight on our hands."

"Oh, no!" wailed Emily, looking at Neil. But Neil just shrugged. He knew there was nothing else they could do.

*   *   *

Mr. and Mrs. Thomson arrived with Digger just before
six. Bob had advised them to bring the puppy, hoping
that the Carters would see how uncomfortable he
made their daughter, and what a good relationship
he had with the Thomsons. Shortly afterward, the
Carters pulled into the courtyard. "Hello, Tinker,"
Mrs. Carter said when she saw Digger. She made no
move to pat him — just stood awkwardly in front of
him. The puppy didn't respond to her at all.

However, to Neil's dismay, Mr. Carter clumsily
snatched Digger up. "Here's your dog," he said, holding the struggling puppy out to Isobel.

"No! I don't *want* him!" Isobel cried, a terrified look
on her face. Mr. Carter reluctantly put Digger down
again. Neil saw the relief on everyone's faces, and
kneeled down quickly to stroke the confused puppy.

"Perhaps Kate should look after Digger while
we're talking," he suggested.

"Good idea. He'll be in very safe hands with her,"
Bob reassured the Thomsons. They nodded, looking
relieved. "Emily," continued Bob, "would you take
Digger to Kate? She's finishing work in Kennel Block
One. I'm sure she wouldn't mind looking after him
for half an hour."

"I'm going with Digger," insisted Sarah.

Emily picked up the puppy and she and Sarah
headed off to find Kate. Everyone else went inside
and found seats in the large kitchen.

Bob Parker cleared his throat. "The pet shop has confirmed that Mrs. Smith did buy the puppy on the day you said," he began.

Mr. Carter shot his wife a triumphant look.

"But as to whether or not you are responsible dog owners . . ." Bob Parker paused and stared hard at Mr. and Mrs. Carter.

"What right do you have —" Mr. Carter began, but a look from his wife silenced him.

"Let him finish," she said quietly.

"I can tell you have no experience handling dogs," Bob said. "I'm not even sure you care that much for them. And before you fly off the handle" — he directed this at Mr. Carter — "let me give you an example of what I mean. My family spent last New Year's in Australia. Now, if Jake, Neil's dog, had gone missing on the day of our departure, we would have given up our flight and our vacation in order to find him. We wouldn't have thought twice about it."

"Little Digger was only a few weeks old when we found him," added Carole. "He'd only just left his mother. To abandon him like that was downright cruel." She spoke calmly, but her voice was cold.

Neil couldn't keep quiet any longer. "I get the impression that Digger was an unwanted present," he blurted out. He knew he'd hit the truth when he saw Mrs. Carter blush and Isobel nod vigorously. Feeling on safe ground, he continued, "And you didn't try very hard to find him because you didn't really want him back."

"Daddy bought me Princess Melinda instead," Isobel said proudly.

Mr. Carter glared at his small daughter.

Gotcha! thought Neil triumphantly.

"Nothing you've said or done has convinced me that you really love Digger," Bob said. "You showed no interest in meeting him again. Any real dog lover would have made a huge fuss over their pup when they found him after he'd been missing for months. But you didn't. It's obvious to me, and to everyone in this room, that you don't really want him. You may have the legal right to this dog, but if you have any human feelings at all, you'll let him stay with the people who really do love him."

Bob Parker paused, surveying the faces in the room.

Neil realized that this was the moment to play his trump card. He directed it at Isobel. "There's something about Digger you should know," he said. "He hates cats. He chases them."

He didn't want to upset Isobel — he just wanted her to make it clear to her parents that taking Digger home would only make her unhappy. "I don't want him to come home with us, Daddy," she said. "He might chase Princess Melinda and frighten her."

"You know how she loves that cat, Brian," Mrs. Carter said.

Mr. Carter looked away from his wife and daughter and cleared his throat. "I didn't want to mention this before," he said, looking rather embarrassed, "but maybe we could talk about you buying Tinker from us."

Mr. Thomson stood up and faced Mr. Carter. "Now we're talking business! How much do you want for him?" he inquired coldly.

"How much is the bone worth?" asked Mr. Carter.

"Nobody knows yet," Neil told them. "Professor Tate's getting it properly valued."

"How long will that take?" Mr. Carter snapped.

"Not long, we hope," Carole said tactfully.

"Well, I guess I'll have to wait," said Mr. Carter impatiently. "If you agree that the money is ours, Mr. Thomson, then you can keep the dog."

"It's a deal!" Mr. Thomson agreed readily.

"I want to go home," Isobel whined, tugging at her father's hand.

Mr. Carter sighed. Suddenly, he looked less aggressive and more human. "OK," he said. "I'm glad the pup's all right and that you're taking good care of him. But he is our dog, and we have a right to the money."

Mrs. Carter smiled at Mrs. Thomson. "We've always preferred cats, really," she admitted. "Perhaps

my mother buying Tinker — I mean, Digger — was
sort of a mistake."

Bob got to his feet. "I'm glad this matter has been
resolved. I'll give your telephone number to Professor Tate. I'm sure she'll be in touch soon."

The Carters left quickly, obviously embarrassed
now that they had admitted their true motive. Once
they had gone, there were cheers in the kitchen.
Sarah brought Digger in, and everyone made a big
fuss over the puppy. Carole opened a bottle of soda,
and they all drank a toast to Digger, for winning the
right to stay with the Thomsons and for finding the
treasure.

"Who needs a new extension? Digger's a real treasure himself!" said Mrs. Thomson fondly.

Carole took the exhausted Sarah up to bed. Just
after the Thomsons had left, the phone rang. Bob
took the call in the study and came back into the
kitchen with an amused expression on his face.

"You'll never guess what," he told Neil and Emily.
"That was Professor Tate. They've done a proper analy-
sis of the bone and it's not real gold — it's what they
call fool's gold. A fake. It looks like the baron was
cheated by his jeweler!"

"Does that mean it's not worth very much?" asked
Neil.

"That's right!" replied his father, and they all burst
out laughing.

"So Mr. Carter won't get a fortune after all!" Emily chuckled. "I'm glad!"

"Oh, and there's a message from Mrs. Mitchell on the answering machine," Bob added. "She wants you to pop in tomorrow morning. She says she's got something to tell you."

At ten o'clock the following morning, Mrs. Mitchell opened the door, her face wreathed in smiles. She was cradling the Dachshund in her arms. "She's a

very clever Banana," she informed them. "I took her to Mike Turner's clinic and it's a good thing I did, because guess what? She's going to be a mom!"

"I don't believe it!" Emily exclaimed.

"She doesn't look as if she's pregnant. But then, some dogs don't show until they're almost ready to have their puppies," Neil said knowledgeably.

"No wonder she wanted more rests than the others," said Emily.

"Yes. She's quite elderly for a first-time mom. Mike says moderate exercise will do her good, so I think I'll just walk her around the block today," she said.

The Thomsons were going on a picnic with Digger, so there were no dogs to walk in Padsham that Tuesday. Neil saw Emily's expression and knew she was thinking about how their birthday present fund would suffer.

They left Banana and Mrs. Mitchell and decided to go up to the castle and tell Vicki the good news about Digger.

They found the professor in the small lecture hall inside the museum. She was standing by the table with two of her students, examining an array of shiny objects. She was delighted to hear that Digger was safe with the Thomsons.

"That's fantastic news. I can't believe how greedy those Carters are!"

"Yeah. Well, they'll be furious when they find out all their efforts were for nothing," laughed Neil.

"And you'll be happy to hear that there's good news about the items that were in the chest," said Professor Tate. "The stones on that collar are definitely rubies, Neil, and the dog statue is studded with sapphires."

Neil whistled in surprise, and he and Emily bent closer to examine their finds.

Professor Tate smiled. "It looks as though they might be very valuable, and since you two and Jake helped to find them, we think it's only fair that you should get a small reward."

She mentioned a sum that took Neil's breath away. *It will pay for a whole wall full of aerial photographs of King Street Kennels,* he thought jubilantly.

"Come and see the progress we've made," Vicki invited them.

They strolled down the hill to the treasure site. A lot of land had been removed, and the foundations of the Norman houses were clearly visible. They stretched from where the golden bone was found over to the area where the dogs had unearthed the silver chest.

Jake jumped down among the ruins and started scratching away in the soil, his front paws flying.

"Jake! Come here!" Neil commanded.

"Not again!" Emily sighed.

The Border collie glanced up, hesitated, then carried on digging. Suddenly, there was a click as Jake's paws struck something metallic. It glinted in the sunlight.

"Vicki! Over here, quick!" Emily called, as Neil clambered down to Jake. "I think Jake's found something else."

The professor ran up and climbed down next to Neil. She picked the object up and examined it. "Hmm. It looks like a medallion — silver, if I'm not mistaken. Here, take a look." She handed it to Neil.

"Look, Em, this is so awesome! It's got a dog on it, and he looks just like Jake!" he said, passing it to his sister.

"There's some funny writing on the other side," Emily observed. "It's the same as the writing on the not-so-golden bone!"

"I think you're right, Emily," said Vicki Tate. "It must have belonged to the baron, too."

I wish it belonged to me, thought Neil longingly.

"I must take it back to be cataloged and photographed, but I don't think it's particularly valuable. Since Jake found it, I don't see why you can't be allowed to keep it," Professor Tate said. "It can be Jake's bravery medal for having gotten rid of Professor Herbert for us."

Who says wishes never come true? Neil thought happily as he smiled his thanks and gave Jake a congratulatory hug. The Thomsons got their wish: Digger now truly belonged to them. The professor got her television series and the credit for the treasure. He and Jake got the medallion — a gift from centuries ago, from one dog lover to another.

And speaking of gifts, he and Emily could now buy their parents the perfect birthday present!